'Thank you for coming to my birthday party, Wibbly Pig. Don't forget your party bag.'

Other Wibbly Pig books

Wibbly Pig likes bananas
Wibbly Pig can dance
Wibbly Pig is happy
Wibbly Pig makes pictures
Wibbly Pig opens his presents
Wibbly Pig makes a tent
Everyone Hide from Wibbly Pig
In Wibbly's Garden
Is it bedtime Wibbly Pig?
Tickly Christmas Wibbly Pig
Wibbly Pig's Silly Big Bear

Don't lose Pigley, Wibbly Pig!

Mick Inkpen

Hodder
Children's
Books

A division of Hachette Children's Books

Wibbly can't open his party bag. He doesn't have any spare hands.

So off he goes with his party bag in one hand, his balloon in the other and Pigley under his arm.

Wibbly can't wait.
He tips out his party bag.
Three things.
A jelly alien.
A licky lolly.
And one Other Thing,
with tricky paper to undo.

He licks his lolly
and wonders about
the Other Thing.
He can't open it.
He can't let go
of his balloon.
And now he has a
sticky, licky lolly.
He can't put that down.

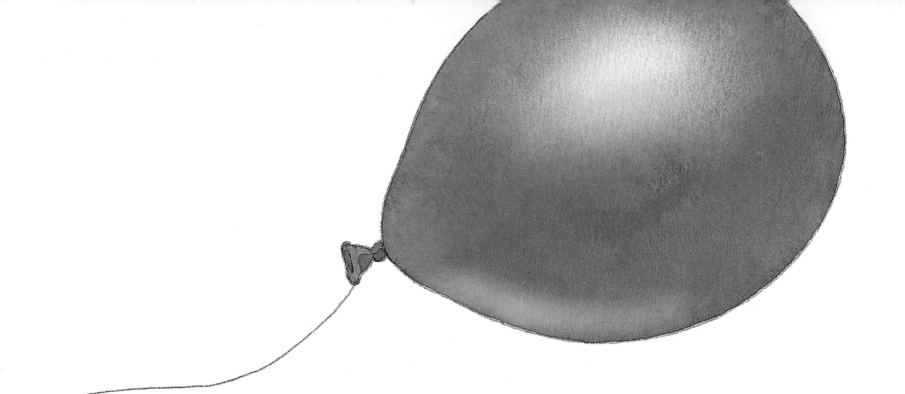

Wibbly can't wait.
He sticks his sticky,
licky lolly in his mouth,
and ties Pigley to the
balloon to stop it
flying away.
Clever Wibbly.

He looks at the
Other Thing.
He shakes it.
He pokes it.
He sniffs it.
He doesn't notice
Pigley floating up. . .

. . . .until it is too late.

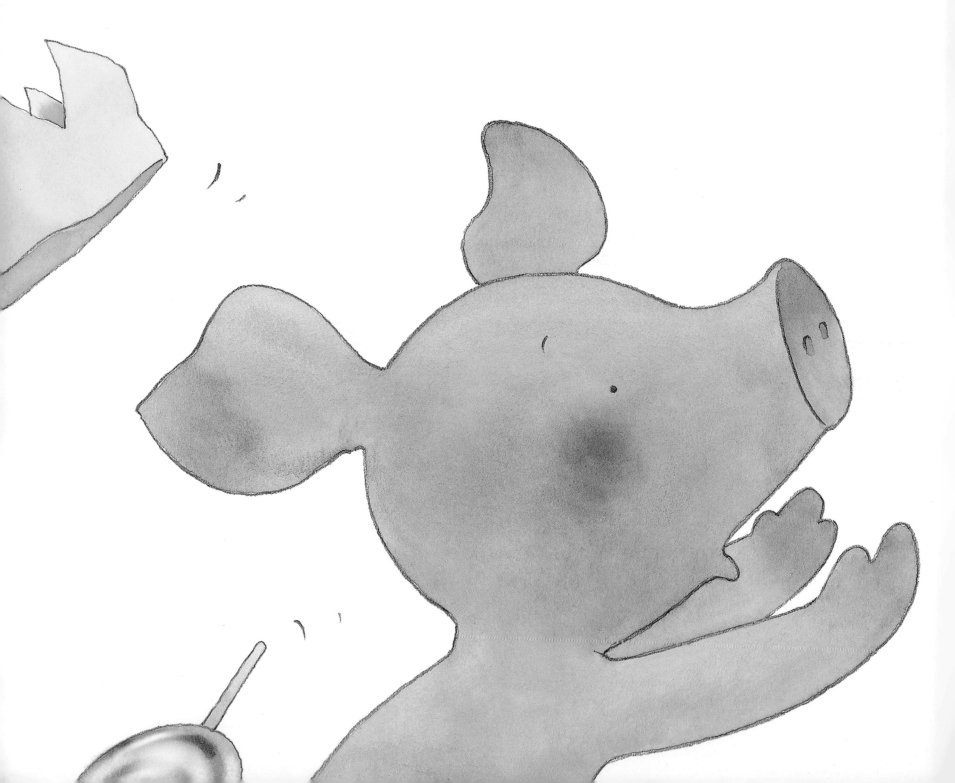

'Come back, Pigley!
Come back!'

He grabs his things,
and chases after
the balloon.
   He can't lose Pigley!
He just can't!

Along the street. Into the park. Over the bridge

And all the way up the hill. But he just can't catch up!

He throws his sticky,
licky lolly after Pigley!
(He doesn't know what else to do.)
It hits the balloon. . .

Down comes the balloon. Down comes the sticky, licky

olly. But where is Pigley?

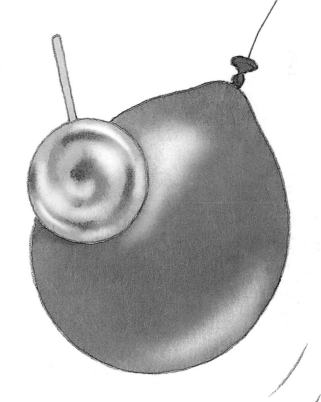

He is stuck on top of
a tall thing.
    Wibbly pulls the string,
very, very, very carefully.
    Pigley seems to wave
goodbye.
    The string
comes undone.
    Oh dear!

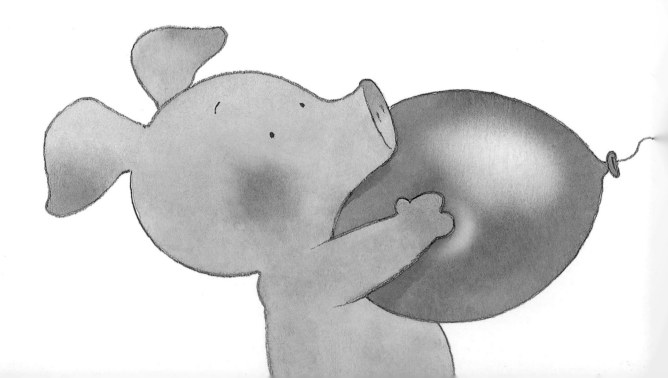

Wibbly can't
get Pigley back.
And he has lost
his jelly alien.
He licks his
sticky, licky lolly.
It tastes rubbery.
He begins to sniff.
He opens the
Other Thing. . .

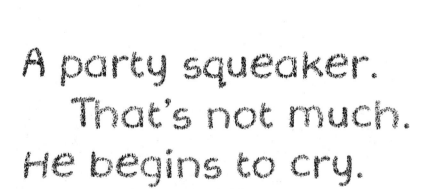

A party squeaker.
That's not much.
He begins to cry.

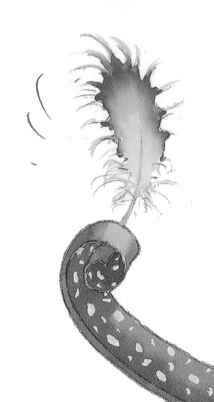

Wibbly blows
his party squeaker.
Pheeep!
It sounds sad too.
But it unrolls
just as it should,
and wiggles
its feather. . .

which gives Wibbly. . .

...a very, very, good

First published in 2009
by Hodder Children's Books

Text and illustrations copyright © Mick Inkpen 2009

Hodder Children's Books
338 Euston Road, London NW1 3BH

Hodder Children's Books Australia
Level 17/207 Kent Street, Sydney, NSW 2000

A catalogue record of this book is
available from the British Library.

ISBN: 978 0 7500 5081 4

Printed in China

Hodder Children's Books is a
division of Hachette Children's Books
An Hachette UK Company
www.hachette.co.uk